Raj
and the
BEST DAY EVER!

For Genevieve and Katie! SB

A TEMPLAR BOOK

First published in the UK in 2018 by Templar Publishing,
an imprint of Kings Road Publishing, part of the Bonnier Publishing Group,
The Plaza, 535 King's Road, London, SW10 0SZ
www.bonnierpublishing.com

ISBN 978-1-78741-234-7

This book was typeset in Providence Sans
The illustrations were created digitally

Edited by Katie Haworth
Designed by Genevieve Webster

Printed in China

templar
books

Raj
and the
BEST DAY EVER!

Seb Braun

Today is going to be the
BEST DAY EVER!
Dad and I are going on an adventure.

We have lots of ideas, so we make a list.

1. Borrow a book from the library
2. Go to the city farm and drive the tractor
3. Watch the boats go up the river
4. Look at pictures in the gallery
5. Go to the café
6. Come home in a lovely bus

"This is a long list," says Dad.
I say that it's the **perfect** length.

Dad and I pack our adventure bag.
"Can you think of anything else we need, Raj?" asks Dad.

I tell him that adventurers need
superhero capes,
and I put mine on.

"It's quite a long way to the library," says Dad. "But look! There is SO much to see!"

He's right! We see lots of things.

When we get to the library we go straight in.
I'm going to choose my **best** book.

OPEN
ALL THE
TIME

Dad tries to guess which one it is.
"Is it a book about a **superhero** by any chance?" he asks.

How does he **always** know?

At the library you need a special card to borrow a book,
so Dad opens his bag.

First he rummages inside, then he tips everything onto the floor and then he says . . .

Outside the library
it has started to rain.
I feel rainy too.
"No wallet means we
can't do the things on
our list," says Dad.

"This is going to be the
WORST DAY EVER,"
I say back.

Soon there is so much rain we have to run for shelter.

But then I see something that gives me a plan . . .

And I show Dad how to drive a
shiny red tractor,
just like the ones at the city farm.

We have **SO** much **fun** we almost don't notice
it's stopped raining.

Next, we walk to the park.
I ask Dad if we have
to go home now, but
he says he has an idea.

PARK

"Raj," he says. "Can you see a leaf, a stick and a piece of bark?"
I look **really** hard and then I do.

Dad shows me how to turn them into a boat . . .

. . . and then we launch it!

I chase it down the stream
until it's sailed away.

"What shall we do now?" I ask.

Dad takes out the list.
"We were going to look at pictures in the gallery."

I look around us. "Maybe there are pictures in the park?"

When I say I'm hungry,
Dad looks at the list again.
"We can't go to the café," he says,
"But we can make our own café
right here."

So we do.

Neither of us
looks at
the list . . .

. . . until . . .

. . . it's
too late.

I am very
annoyed.

The list is stuck
in a tall tree.
"If we don't have
the list we won't
know what to do!"
I say.

If I could **fly** like a
SUPERHERO
I could get it down.

Luckily Dad is good at **helping**.

But then, when I'm about to save the day,
something **terrible** happens.

A bird steals our list and flies away! "What a **cheeky** bird," says Dad.

WHOOSH

Dad tells me not to worry.
"Think about all the **lovely** things we have done, Raj!"

I think **really** hard. "I still remember what was
on the list," I say. "We were going to catch a lovely bus."
"I can be your lovely bus," says Dad.

But I have a **better** idea.

"You can be my
Superhero Dad
instead!"

"Let's fly home!"
says Dad.

"NO WALLET,
NO BUS,
NO BRAIN,
GOOD LEGS!"

Finally, we make it home.
"Have you got your keys, Dad?" I say.

Dad looks in his bag. Then he rummages inside.
Then he turns it upside down. I don't see any keys.

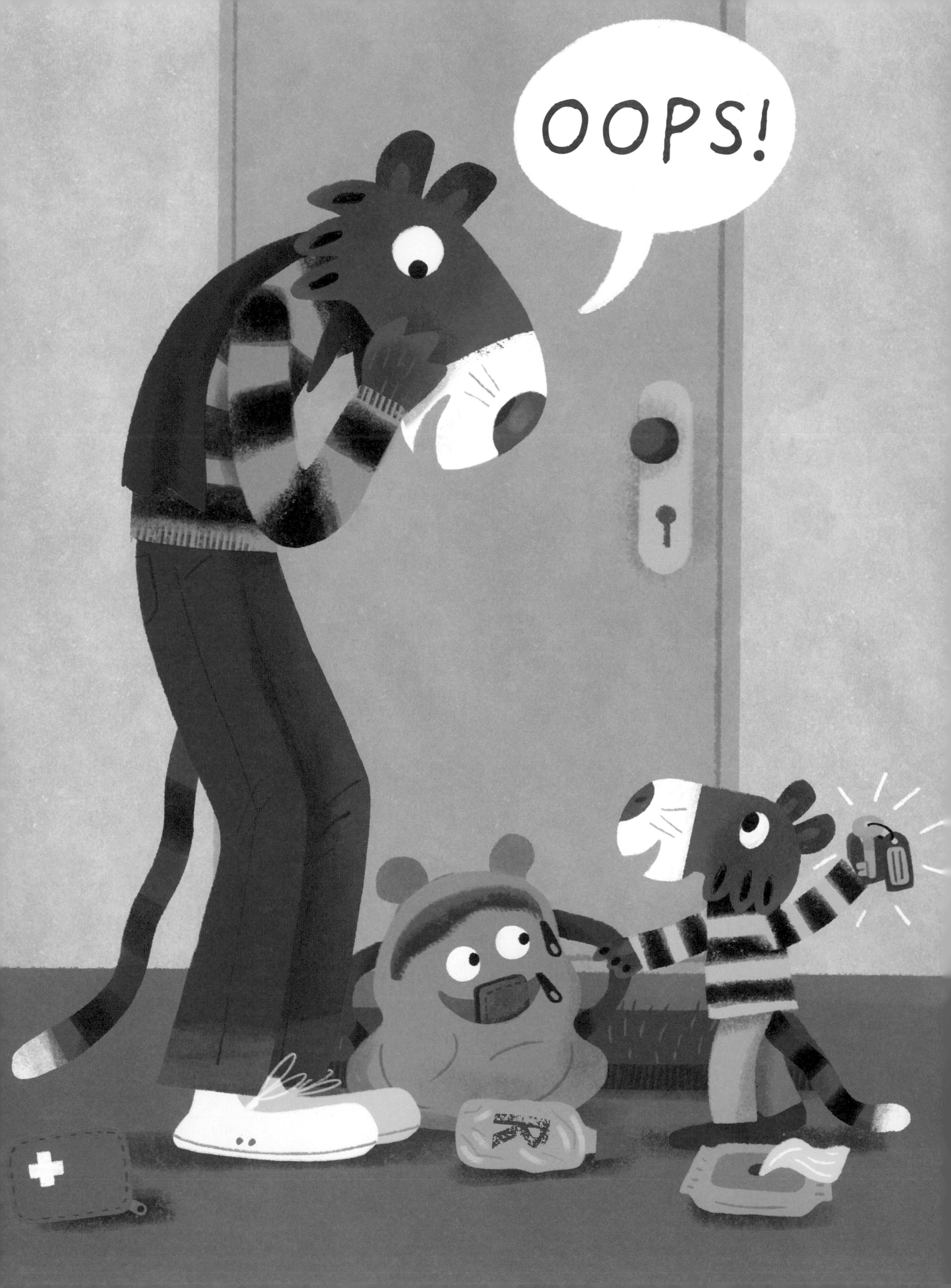
OOPS!

The end!

More picture books from Templar:

ISBN: 978-1-78370-833-8

ISBN: 978-1-78370-801-7

ISBN: 978-1-78741-008-4 (hardback)
978-1-78370-140-7 (paperback)

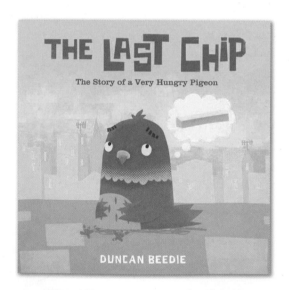

ISBN: 978-1-78370-001-1 (hardback)
978-1-78370-062-2 (paperback)